DORLING KINDERSLEY *CLASSICS*

OLIVER TWIST

Dorling Kindersley

LONDON, NEW YORK, SYDNEY, DELHI,
PARIS, MUNICH and JOHANNESBURG

A RETELLING FOR YOUNG READERS

Produced by Leapfrog Press Ltd
Project Editor Naia Bray-Moffatt
Art Editor Penny Lamprell

For DK Publishing
Senior Editor Alastair Dougall
Managing Art Editor Jacquie Gulliver
Picture Research Frances Vargo
Production Steve Lang
US Editors Lilan Patri, Connie Robinson

Published in the United States by Dorling Kindersley Publishing, Inc.
95 Madison Avenue, New York, New York 10016

First American Edition 1999
Paperback edition published in 2000
2 4 6 8 10 9 7 5 3 1

Library of Congress Cataloging-in-Publication Data
Bray-Moffatt, Naia.
    Oliver Twist/by Charles Dickens ; adapted by Naia Bray-Moffatt.-- 1st American ed.
        p. cm. -- (Dorling Kindersley read and listen)
    Includes an audio tape featuring a reading of the text with special effects and music.
    Summary: Retells the adventures of the orphan boy who is forced to practice thievery
and live a life of crime in nineteenth-century London. Illustrated notes throughout the
text explain the historical background of the story.
    ISBN: 0-7894-5463-7 (pb & tape)
    [1. Orphans--Fiction. 2. Robbers and outlaws--Fiction. 3. London (England)--Fiction.]
1. Dickens, Charles, 1812-1870. Oliver Twist. II. Title. III. Series.
PZ7.B73887 O1 2000
[Fic]--dc21   99-050014

Color reproduction by Bright Arts
Printed and bound in China by L.Rex Printing Co., Ltd.

For our complete
catalog visit
www.dk.com

DORLING KINDERSLEY CLASSICS

Oliver Twist

Charles Dickens

Illustrated by
Ian Andrew

Adapted by
Naia Bray-Moffatt

A Dorling Kindersley Book

Oliver Twist

The artful Dodger

Fagin

Bill Sikes

CONTENTS

Nancy

Mr. Brownlow

Mr. Bumble

Monks

INTRODUCTION

WRITTEN IN 1837, *Oliver Twist* is one of the best known of Charles Dickens's books. Subtitled *"The Parish Boy's Progress,"* it is the earliest novel in the English language that has a child as its main character. But the novel is not just about the fortunes of the young orphan boy Oliver Twist. It is filled with memorable characters many of whom seem more real than the hero himself. For Oliver is a passive character, a mirror reflecting the innocence and corruption he meets. Through his eyes the reader experiences the different ways of life and society in early Victorian days, from the frightening world of the criminal underclass to the comfortable world of the well-to-do.

The London underworld fascinated the Victorians, and crime reports and stories about murderers and other criminals were very popular. Although Dickens wanted to entertain his audience, he also wanted to highlight how desperation drove many, including children, to crime. Many of his readers at the time were surprised at the seriousness of the novel – Dickens's first book, *The Pickwick Papers*, was a comedy. But they were not disappointed. *Oliver Twist* sold well and even young Queen Victoria is said to have enjoyed it!

Oliver Twist remains popular today, both because of its exciting story and its wealth of superbly drawn characters, many of whom live on in the imagination long after the book has been finished.

Dickens brings London's crowded streets vividly to life.

CHILDREN AND CRIME

Many children earned their living on the streets.

For children of poor parents, life in Victorian cities was extremely hard. They faced a choice of long hours of dangerous work in the factories, begging on the streets, or life in a workhouse, a government-run home for the poor. The alternative was a life of crime. A report published by Henry Mayhew 20 years after *Oliver Twist* was written estimated that 12,000 people in London considered crime a career. Dickens was concerned about the corrupting influence of thieves on poor children who had no one else to look up to. In many ways the reader sympathizes with the character of the artful Dodger, who steals to gain independence and the chance of a better life. But the punishments he risks are terrible, as Oliver discovers, and the ultimate conclusion of *Oliver Twist* is that crime doesn't pay.

Living conditions
In the 19th century many people moved from the countryside to find work in the cities. There were no proper houses for them to live in, and the slum areas that developed were dirty and unhealthy. Disease spread quickly in such overcrowded conditions, and many children died.

Children sit under a clothesline in a London slum.

A boy sweeps while his friend collects the money.

Crossing sweeper
Victorian streets were full of mud and horse manure. A common job for children was to sweep a path so that ladies and gentlemen could cross.

CHILD EMPLOYMENT
In the first half of the 19th century there were very few laws to protect working children. It was not required for children to attend school, so some children were sent to work as young as five or six. Being small, they were made to do jobs such as crawling underneath factory machines or climbing narrow chimneys, no matter how dangerous. It was common for children to work 12 hours a day, and they might be beaten if they didn't work hard enough. Dickens himself was sent to work in a blacking factory, labeling shoe polish, instead of attending school.

A young chimney sweep, face blackened with soot

Learning a trade

Boys from workhouses, like Oliver, were apprenticed to a master to learn a useful trade. Some children were lucky and had good masters. But others were treated badly and made to work very hard in return for little more than a roof over their heads. Oliver's unhappy experience with Mr. Sowerberry, the undertaker, was typical of many children who were not allowed to choose the trade they were to learn.

This young boy is apprenticed to a chimney sweep.

Training a pickpocket

Picking pockets could be very lucrative. Children as young as six or seven were trained to steal by older thieves, just as Fagin trains his gang of boys to steal in the book. One training method was to hang up a coat with a bell attached to it. A child would have to take the handkerchief from the pocket without ringing the bell.

A boy practices picking a pocket.

LAW AND ORDER

A Victorian policeman

At the time that Dickens wrote Oliver Twist, *policemen in London had been on the streets for less than ten years. Before that the city and the rest of the country relied either on unpaid parish constables or on the army if there were riots. It was not until 1856 that every town was required to have a police force. The laws punishing criminals were very severe, but soon changes were made. The death penalty for 200 offenses was abolished, but Dickens was appalled by the public hangings which continued to be held until 1868.*

Robert Peel

Sir Robert Peel, Britain's Home Secretary (responsible for law and order), created the Metropolitan Police Act, which is why the new policemen became known as "bobbies" or "peelers."

A pair of handcuffs

Peelers

The first policemen appeared on the streets of London on September 29, 1829. They wore tailcoats and top hats and instead of being armed they carried short wooden batons, or sticks, under their tailcoats.

A new arrival at Newgate prison

Prisons

When hanging was abolished for most crimes during the 19th century, imprisonment was used as punishment instead. Prisoners were treated very harshly so that they would be afraid to commit crimes again. Usually locked up in cells by themselves, criminal prisoners were only allowed out to do "hard labor" for hours every day. Dickens, whose own father was imprisoned for debt at Marshalsea prison in London, wrote about it in his book, *Little Dorrit*.

A whipping post

Punishment

Punishment in prison was severe and included the treadmill, a revolving cylinder with a series of steps on which the prisoner was forced to walk, and the whipping post. Victims were strapped to a wooden post so they could not move, and then beaten with a whip. In some cases the beating was so bad the victim died.

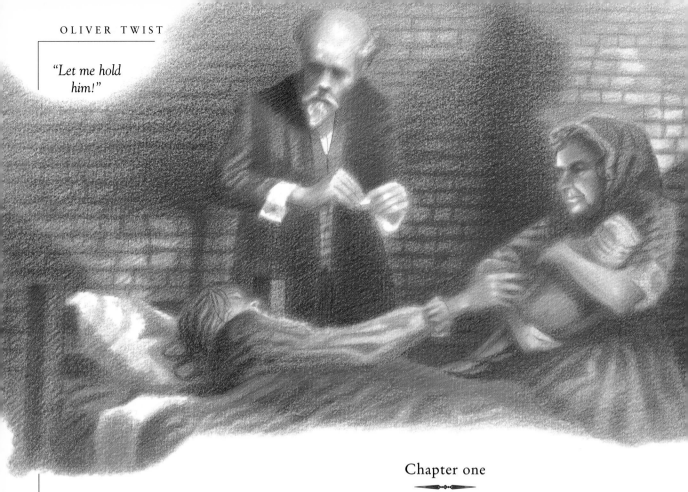

"Let me hold him!"

Workhouse life
A workhouse was a government-run home for the poor. Men, women, boys, and girls lived in separate parts. Life was deliberately made hard so that people would only go there as a last resort.

Chapter one

BORN IN THE WORKHOUSE

ON A COLD AND WET NIGHT a young woman was found lying in the street. You could tell she had walked a long way, for her shoes were as thin and worn out as she was, and though she was about to have a baby, she had no wedding ring. No one knew anything else about her – neither where she had come from, nor where she was going.

This poor young girl was taken into the workhouse, and there she had her baby. "Let me hold him," she whispered. When the surgeon put the boy in her arms she pressed her cold white lips passionately on his forehead, then fell back – and died. Oliver Twist was an orphan.

As there was no one who could look after a baby in the workhouse, Oliver was sent to a nursery to be looked after by an elderly woman called Mrs. Mann. In truth, Mrs. Mann was fonder of looking after herself than the children in her care.

There was never enough food and always too many beatings, but at least Oliver had friends, and he knew nothing else.

And so it was that on Oliver's ninth birthday, he found himself with two of these friends – locked in the coal cellar for daring to be hungry – when Mr. Bumble, the beadle in charge of the workhouse, unexpectedly paid a visit.

"Goodness gracious! Mr. Bumble, how glad I am to see you, surely!" said Mrs. Mann. She gestured to the maid to unlock the boys and quickly wash them, and showed Mr. Bumble into the parlor.

"Oliver Twist is nine years old today," began Mr. Bumble.

"Bless him!" said Mrs. Mann.

"And despite a most generous reward of ten pounds, we have never been able to discover anything about his family."

Mrs. Mann raised her hands in astonishment, before adding, "How comes he to have any name at all then?"

The beadle drew himself up with great pride and said, "I invented it. We name our orphans in alphabetical order. The last was an S – Swubble, I named him. This was a T – Twist, I called him. And this Twist is now too old to stay here. I have come out myself to take him back to the workhouse, so let me see him at once."

"I'll fetch him immediately," said Mrs. Mann. And Oliver, having by this time been well scrubbed, was presented.

"Will you go along with me, Oliver?" said Mr. Bumble in a majestic voice, as if Oliver had any choice, which he didn't. So Oliver found himself waving good-bye to his companions of nine years and trotting along to keep up with the long strides of Mr. Bumble on his way to the workhouse.

Beadle
A beadle was a minor Victorian official with some powers to punish minor offenses. The most impressive thing about him was his uniform.

"Will you go along with me, Oliver?"

Picking oakum
This involved unraveling lengths of old rope into strands which could be rewoven into a loose fiber called oakum. It was used to plug up leaks, particularly in ships, and to dress wounds.

Gruel
One bowl of gruel, a watered down form of porridge, would not have been filling.

As soon as they arrived, Oliver was taken into a room where eight or ten fat gentlemen sat around a table.

"Bow to the board," said Bumble. Seeing no board but the table, Oliver luckily bowed to that. But the sight of so many gentlemen made him tremble, and he was unable to answer their questions without crying.

"Well, boy," said one red-faced gentleman, "you have come here to be taught a useful trade. So you'll begin to pick oakum tomorrow morning at six o'clock." Oliver bowed again and was then hurried away to a large ward where, on a rough, hard bed he cried himself to sleep.

The room in which the boys were fed was a large stone hall, with a large, metal container at one end, out of which the master ladled the gruel at mealtimes. Each boy had one bowl of gruel and no more – except on festive days when they were also allowed a small portion of bread.

"Please, sir, I want some more."

Oliver Twist and his companions suffered the torture of slow starvation for three months. At last, it became too much for one boy who was tall for his age. "If I don't get more to eat soon I'll be forced to eat the boy who sleeps next to me. I will, you know." The other boys believed him, and it was clear that someone would have to ask for more food. The boys drew lots to decide who should do this, and Oliver picked the short straw.

That evening the boys took their usual places. The master doled out their gruel, and when the boys had finished eating (which was not very much later) they began to whisper to each other, nudging and winking at Oliver. Nervous, but desperately hungry, Oliver stood up and walked towards the master: "Please, sir, I want some more."

The master turned pale. He looked at the small boy in astonishment.

"What?" he said at last, in a faint voice.

"Please, sir," replied Oliver. "I want some more."

The master hit Oliver with the ladle and shouted for the beadle.

The board were sitting in their room when Mr. Bumble rushed in.

"Begging your pardon gentlemen!" he said. "Oliver Twist has asked for more!"

There was a general start, and a look of horror crossed their faces.

"For more!" said Mr. Limbkins. "Do I understand that he asked for more, after he had eaten his supper?"

"He did, sir," replied Bumble.

"That boy will hang," said the gentleman.

Nobody disputed this, and they all began talking at once. Oliver was ordered into instant confinement, and the next morning a poster was pasted on the outside of the gate, offering a reward of five pounds to anybody who would take Oliver Twist off the hands of the workhouse.

Notes, which we call bills, were cut in two before mailing and sent in separate envelopes for security.

£5 note
Oliver is for sale for £5 (worth approximately $280 today). He has no more rights than a slave.

Funeral processions
*Funeral carriages were pulled
by horses wearing black
plumes, or feathers.*

Chapter two

AMONG THE COFFINS

IT WAS NOT LONG BEFORE someone was found. Business was looking up for Mr. Sowerberry, the parish undertaker. Never before had he known so many funerals, and if he hadn't had such a naturally gloomy face he might almost have looked happy. But he needed an extra pair of hands, and it didn't take long for the board to agree that Oliver should be apprenticed to him.

"Dear me!" said the undertaker's wife, when she inspected the boy. "He's very small. Still, I suppose he'll grow on our food and drink. But men always thinks they knows best."

There! Get downstairs, you little bag of bones."

With that, Mrs. Sowerberry opened a side door, and pushed Oliver down a steep flight of stairs into a damp stone cell, where a grubby-looking girl was sitting.

"Here, Charlotte," said Mrs. Sowerberry who had followed Oliver down, "give the boy some of the cold bits that were put by for the dog. And then show him where to sleep. You don't mind sleeping among the coffins?" she asked, turning to Oliver. "There's nowhere else anyway, so it don't make any odds if you *do* mind."

You may well imagine that Oliver did mind being left alone to sleep among the coffins. As Oliver lay down on his narrow bed he found himself wishing that it was his coffin, and that he might go to sleep and never wake up.

Wake up he did though, and for the next few weeks his sad expression – for he did not have much to be happy about – gave Mr. Sowerberry the idea that he would make a perfect mute. "I don't mean a regular mute to attend grown-up people, my dear," he explained to his wife. "But only for children's funerals. It would have a superb effect."

"You don't mind sleeping among the coffins?"

Oliver gained a great deal of experience very quickly, and his success surpassed even Mr. Sowerberry's hopes. But this success, so pleasing to Mr. Sowerberry, was not to Noah Claypole. As a charity boy who had worked for the undertaker for some time, Noah felt his status should put him above that of a common workhouse boy. He had endured the taunts of the more fortunate local boys for long enough. It was his right now to be superior to Oliver. That Oliver had been promoted, so successfully, to a mute, wearing a hat band and carrying a black stick while he remained stationary in muffin cap and leathers was unbearable. And Noah never failed to treat Oliver badly as a result.

Charity boys
Some boys from poor families attended charity schools, which provided a basic education. They were made to wear a distinctive uniform, and Noah is proud of the status this gives him.

Mute
Mutes were trained to march alongside the coffin at funerals. This display of grief that could be bought reveals the hypocrisy of many Victorians, who cared more about show than real emotion.

15

Mrs. Sowerberry rushed
into the kitchen.

An ornate coffin

Coffin
*Rich Victorians liked to
display their wealth as much
in death as in life, with
ornate and costly coffins.
Paupers were buried without
a coffin and thrown into a
grave with other bodies.*

One day, Oliver
and Noah were alone in
the kitchen, when Noah
decided to have another go at baiting
Oliver. First Noah pulled Oliver's hair, and then he tweaked his ears
and pinched him and called him names. Oliver didn't react at all,
which annoyed Noah even more. He was determined to
make Oliver cry.

"Work'us," said Noah. "How's your mother?"

"She's dead," replied Oliver; "don't you say anything
about her to me!"

Oliver's face turned red as he said this and Noah, delighted to
have got some reaction at last, carried on.

"What did she die of, Work'us?"

"Of a broken heart, some of the nurses told me," replied Oliver,
breathing heavily.

"Well I've heard yer mother was a regular right-down bad 'un."

"What did you say?" asked Oliver, looking up quickly.

"A regular right-down bad 'un, Work'us," replied Noah coolly. "And it's a good thing she died when she did or she'd be in prison by now, or transported, or hung more likely."

Oliver could control himself no more. He jumped up and took Noah by the throat, shaking him so hard his teeth rattled, and then with all the strength left in him, he hit Noah an almighty blow, knocking him to the ground.

"He'll murder me!" screamed Noah. "Charlotte! Missis! The new boy's murdering me. Help! Help!"

Charlotte and Mrs. Sowerberry rushed into the kitchen and seeing Noah lying on the floor, they both seized Oliver and began hitting him and scratching him before throwing him into the cellar and locking him up.

"Oh Charlotte!" cried Mrs. Sowerberry. "It's a wonder we've not been murdered in our beds. Poor Noah. All but killed and the master not at home. Quick, Noah, run to Mr. Bumble and tell him to come as fast as he can."

Oliver was still kicking the cellar door when Noah returned with Mr. Bumble carrying his cane. But the sound of Mr. Bumble's impressive voice did not quiet him or make him repentant. Even when Mr. Sowerberry returned and Oliver was let out of the cellar, he did not calm down.

"He called my mother names," explained Oliver.

"Well, and what if he did?" said Mrs. Sowerberry. "She deserved what he said, and worse."

"She didn't," said Oliver. "It's a lie."

This rudeness to his wife left Mr. Sowerberry no alternative but to punish Oliver severely. He was beaten and then shut up in the back kitchen for the rest of the day with nothing to eat until bedtime, when he went to sleep among the coffins.

Prisoners awaiting transportation from Chatham Dockyard, Kent, 1828

Transportation
Noah is very cruel to suggest that Oliver's mother would have been transported. Transportation, where criminals as young as 15 were sent by ship to Australia (then a British colony), was a severe punishment.

"He called my mother names."

He took the first road he could see.

London traffic
Although there were no cars in Victorian London, horse-drawn traffic was very heavy. The noise was said to be so loud you could hear it even inside the thick walls of St Paul's Cathedral.

Chapter three

THE DODGER AND THE MISER

THAT NIGHT, alone and in the silence of the undertaker's shop, Oliver at last allowed himself to cry. For a long time he hid his face in his hands and wept. But finally, when he stopped, he had come to a decision. He got up and as quietly as possible, undid the bolts on the door and walked out into the cold, dark night.

He didn't know where he was going but took the first road he could see and began to run. When daylight broke he hid behind hedges, and it was not until noon that day that he allowed himself to rest and to think where he should try to live.

London seemed the best place to try – no one could find him in such a big place – not even Mr. Bumble, and a signpost had said it was only seventy miles away. With renewed enthusiasm, Oliver set off again.

Seventy miles is a long way to walk even if you have lots of food and drink. And Oliver had neither. But somehow, by begging and pleading, Oliver managed to find enough food to keep him going so that by the morning of the seventh day he was limping, cold and sore, into Barnet, a town on the outskirts of the big city. It was still early and most of the streets were empty so Oliver sat down on a doorstep, too tired to walk any further. He stayed there for quite some time, watching the city wake up and the coaches passing by, when he noticed a boy looking at him. He paid no attention to begin with but as the boy kept on staring, Oliver at

"Me friends call me 'the artful Dodger.'"

last returned his gaze. Seeing this, the boy crossed the street and said to him: "Hello! What's the row?"

The boy was about Oliver's age but one of the oddest looking boys he'd ever seen. He was snub-nosed, dirty, and small, with bowlegs and sharp, ugly eyes but he had all the airs and graces of a grown-up. He wore a man's coat that was much too big for him and corduroy trousers with deep pockets.

"I'm very hungry and tired," Oliver replied at last, trying not to cry. "I've walked a long way for seven days."

"Walking for sivin days? My! My! Got any lodgings?"

"No."

"Money?"

"No."

The strange boy whistled and put his arms into his pockets as far as they would go.

"Well, don't fret your eyelids. I know a 'spectable old genelman as lives in London, wot'll give you lodgings for nothink, and never ask for the change – that is, if any genelman he knows inerduces you. The name's Jack Dawkins, by the way. But me friends call me 'the artful Dodger.'"

Oliver could hardly believe his luck.

Barnet
Barnet lay on the main route into London. In Oliver's time it was a small town. Now it is part of north London.

*Oliver and his new friend
arrived in London.*

Fagin
*The character of Fagin was
based on Ikey Solomon, a
well-known criminal.*

Clay pipes
*In the 19th century, many
people smoked tobacco in
clay pipes. Clay was a good,
cheap material from which
to make a pipe, and did
not spoil the flavor of
the tobacco.*

It was after eleven o' clock at night when Oliver and his new friend arrived at Saffron Hill in the heart of London's city.

The narrow streets were so filthy and foul-smelling that Oliver was just thinking about running away again when the Dodger pushed open a door and pulled Oliver into a passage.

"Who's that?" cried a voice from below.

"Plummy and Slam!" replied the Dodger.

This seemed to be some sort of password, for the light of a candle gleamed at the end of the passage and a man's face peeped out.

"There's two of you," he said. "Who's the t'other one?"

"A new pal," said the Dodger, pulling Oliver forward.

They climbed some broken stairs into a dark and dirty back-room. Four or five boys were sitting round a table, smoking clay pipes and drinking like middle-aged men. Some sausages were cooking on the fire, and standing over them was a very old and wicked-looking man whose ugly face was partly hidden by a mass of red hair. The Dodger whispered something to the old man and then turned and grinned at Oliver.

"This is him, Fagin," said the Dodger, "my friend, Oliver Twist."

Fagin grinned and made a low bow. "We are very glad to see you, Oliver, very," he said. "Dodger, bring a seat for Oliver near the fire. Ah, I see you're staring at the pocket-handkerchiefs, eh, my dear! There are a lot, ain't there? We've just got them out to wash, that's all. Ha! ha! ha!"

The other boys joined in the noisy laughter, and then they went to supper. Oliver ate his share and drank a glass of hot gin and water which Fagin gave him. Soon after, he felt himself gently lifted onto a sack where he sank into a deep sleep.

When Oliver woke the next morning everyone had gone except Fagin who was making coffee in a saucepan. He was not yet properly awake so that when Fagin called his name, Oliver didn't reply.

Very quietly Fagin took out a small box from a hiding place in the floor. His eyes glistened as he opened the lid and fingered the

contents: a magnificent gold watch, rings, brooches and many other beautiful pieces of jewelry.

Suddenly Fagin saw that Oliver was watching him. He slammed the lid shut, and picking up the bread knife from the table, demanded furiously, "How long have you been awake? What have you seen? Speak out boy! Quick – quick!"

"Not long, sir. I'm very sorry, sir," replied Oliver meekly.

"Did you see any of these pretty things, my dear?"

"Yes, sir."

"Ah!" said Fagin, turning rather pale. "They're mine, Oliver, my little property. All I have to live upon in my old age. The folks call me a miser, my dear. That's all."

"This is him, Fagin," said the Dodger, "my friend, Oliver Twist."

Diamond brooch

Sapphire earrings

Jewelry
Expensive jewelry, often intricately designed as here, was worn by wealthy women on special occasions. Diamonds and sapphires were particularly popular.

Fagin and the two boys played a very curious game.

Finely worked silver

Snuff

Snuff box
Powdered tobacco, called snuff, was sniffed by Victorian gentlemen to clear the nose. Snuff was kept in valuable silver boxes, like this one, small enough to fit into a gentleman's pocket.

Oliver went to wash, and by the time he had finished, the Dodger had returned with one of the boys from the night before, Charley Bates.

"I hope you've been at work this morning, my dears?" said Fagin.

"Hard," replied the Dodger, producing two beautifully made wallets. Fagin looked pleased. Then Charley took out four pocket-handkerchiefs.

"Well," said Fagin, after inspecting them closely. "They're very good ones, very. Would you like to be able to make handkerchiefs as easy as Charley, my dear?" Fagin said, turning to Oliver.

"Very much, indeed, if you'll teach me, sir," replied Oliver which, to Oliver's surprise, made Master Bates laugh so much he nearly choked.

After breakfast, Fagin and the two boys played a very curious game. Fagin placed a snuff box in one trouser pocket, a wallet in the other, and a watch in his waistcoat pocket. Then he trotted up and down the room with a stick pretending to be a grand gentleman taking a walk. The two boys followed closely, hiding quickly every time Fagin turned round. At last the Dodger trod upon the old man's toes, while Charley stumbled against him. And in that moment, quick as a flash, they took from him the various contents of his pockets.

When they had played this game many times, a couple of young ladies arrived. Bet and Nancy were both rather untidy and not exactly pretty, but Oliver liked them. They stayed a long time and had a few drinks before Charley suggested the four of them go out.

"It's a nice life, isn't it, Oliver?" said Fagin when they were alone. "Now, see if you can take my handkerchief out of my pocket without my feeling it."

Fagin was delighted when Oliver succesfully produced the handkerchief. "You'll be the greatest man of our time," he said patting Oliver on the head.

Oliver couldn't think what playing a funny game had to do with becoming a great man but supposed that the old gentleman must know best.

For many days Oliver stayed in the dark room, sometimes picking the embroidered initials out of handkerchiefs with a needle as he had been shown, and sometimes playing the pocket game. But Oliver longed for fresh air and the outdoors, and he begged Fagin to be allowed to go out and work with the Dodger and Charley Bates.

At last, one morning, Fagin decided to grant Oliver's wish, and Oliver was told he might go with his friends. The three boys set out; the Dodger with his coat sleeves tucked up, as usual; Master Bates sauntering along with his hands in his pockets; and Oliver between them wondering where they were going and what work they were going to do.

The three boys set out.

Chapter four

STOP THIEF!

Gone shopping
Shopping was done at the market or at small specialized shops. Shoppers were good targets for pickpockets who could easily slip away unnoticed into the crowds.

THE DODGER and Charley strolled so slowly through the streets that Oliver began to wonder if they were going to do any work at all. The Dodger had a nasty habit of pulling the caps off the heads of small boys, and Charley casually pilfered apples and onions from the market stalls they passed. Oliver was just thinking of going back to Fagin's, when the Dodger suddenly stopped.

"See that gent at the bookstall?" he said to Charley. "He'll do."

Not knowing what they were talking about, Oliver

The Dodger took out a handkerchief.

watched in amazement as the two boys walked stealthily across the road towards the gentleman. Then to his horror, the Dodger plunged his hand into the old gentleman's pocket and took out a handkerchief; he handed it to Charley, and then they both ran away round the corner at top speed.

Suddenly the whole mystery of the handkerchiefs, and the watch, and the jewels, and Fagin became clear. Oliver stood for a moment, the blood tingling through his veins. Then, confused and frightened, he started to run as fast he could.

"Stop thief! Stop thief!"

At that same moment, the old gentleman, realizing his handkerchief was gone, turned round. Seeing Oliver running away, he immediately chased after him, the book still in his hand, shouting "Stop thief!"

The Dodger and Bates, unwilling to attract attention, had merely stepped into a doorway. They heard the cry and saw Oliver running, and shouted "Stop thief!" too, joining in the chase like good citizens.

"Stop thief! Stop thief!" There was magic in the sound. The shopkeeper left his counter, the butcher threw down his tray, the milkman his pail. Away they ran, helter-skelter, yelling, screaming and the streets echoed with the sound.

Like an animal being hunted, Oliver ran panting with exhaustion, straining to escape his pursuers who were gaining upon him every instant.

Stopped at last! He was down upon the pavement; and the crowd eagerly gathered round him, struggling to catch a glimpse.

Oliver lay, covered with mud and dust, and bleeding from the mouth, looking wildly round at the faces surrounding him.

"Yes," said the gentleman, "I am afraid this is the boy."

A police officer (who is generally the last person to arrive in such cases) at that moment seized Oliver by the collar.

"It wasn't me, sir," Oliver cried, passionately. "It was two other boys. They must be here somewhere."

"Oh no, they ain't," said the officer. This was true, as the Dodger and Charley Bates had slipped away down a convenient lane. "Come on, get up!"

The officer dragged Oliver along, and the gentleman walked with them.

Policemen
Before British policemen were equipped with helmets in 1864, they wore tall, hard hats. These were strong enough to stand on so policemen could look over walls.

Oliver was taken to the nearest police station and locked up in a cell. The old gentleman looked almost as sad as Oliver when the key turned in the lock. "There's something in the boy's face," he said to himself thoughtfully, "something that touches me. He reminds me of someone, but who can it be?" He searched his memory, calling up face after face before his mind's eye. "No," he sighed, shaking his head, "it must be my imagination." Burying his head in his book, he sat down to wait for Oliver's case to be heard.

He did not have to wait long. Oliver was soon brought, trembling, before the magistrate Mr. Fang, a thin, balding man with a red face from too much drink. He was also very bad-tempered.

"Who are you?" he said, scowling at the old gentleman.

"My name, sir, is Brownlow."

"Officer!" said Mr. Fang. "What's the fellow charged with?"

"He's not charged at all, your worship. He is accusing this boy of pickpocketing," the officer replied, pointing at Oliver.

Oliver looked so pale and so ill, and Mr. Brownlow was by now so sure that he could not be guilty, that he tried to explain to the magistrate that he had not actually seen

"What's the fellow charged with?"

Oliver steal anything. But Mr. Fang refused to listen, and when Oliver failed to speak up for himself – being too confused and faint – he sentenced him all the same.

"He stands committed for three months – hard labor, of course."

The room was about to be cleared when an elderly man rushed in. "Stop, stop! Don't take him away!" he cried breathlessly. "I saw it all. I keep the bookstall. You must hear me."

Very reluctantly, Mr. Fang heard the details of the robbery and how the bookseller had seen two other boys steal Mr. Brownlow's handkerchief. He had no choice but to release Oliver.

Outside, Mr. Brownlow was on the point of going home when he saw Oliver. He was bathed in sweat, his face was a deadly white and his whole body was trembling.

"Poor boy, poor boy!" said Mr. Brownlow, bending over him. "Call a coach, somebody, quickly."

A coach arrived, and having carefully laid Oliver on one seat, the old gentleman got in and the two of them were driven away. It took them to Mr. Brownlow's neat house in a shady street near Pentonville. Here, Oliver was at once taken to bed where for many days he lay ill with a fever, unaware of the kindness that was at last being shown to him.

Magistrate
When a criminal was taken to court for the first time his case would be heard by a magistrate (a lower-level judge). In minor cases, such as Oliver's, the magistrate could decide on punishment.

*The man who
spoke was stoutly
built.*

As soon as Oliver had been caught, the Dodger and Charley ran
as fast they could through a maze of narrow streets until, out of
breath, they reached Fagin's house.

Fagin was sitting over the fire with a sausage and a small loaf
in his left hand and a pewter pot on the trivet, when they opened
the door.

"Where's Oliver? Where's the boy?" he demanded
with a menacing look. And when neither
boy replied, Fagin seized the Dodger
by the collar. "Speak out or I'll
throttle you."

"The police have got him," said the
Dodger sullenly. "Now, let me go." And
he slipped out of his big coat, leaving it
empty in Fagin's hands. Fagin picked up
the pot and hurled it in the direction of
the boy. It narrowly missed a man who
was just coming in through the door.

"What the blazes is going on?"
growled the man. "What's this all
about, Fagin?"

The man who spoke was
stoutly built and aged about
thirty-five. He wore a black
velvet coat, dirty breeches, a
brown hat, and a soiled Belcher
handkerchief tied round his neck
with which he wiped beer from his
face. His chin sported a beard of
three day's growth, and he had
clearly been in a recent fight,
for one of his scowling eyes
was black and swollen. A
white dog, with a scratched
and torn face, skulked in
after him. The man kicked

the dog into a corner, where he lay quietly, obviously used to such treatment.

"What's going on?" repeated the man. Fagin looked nervously at Bill Sikes as the boys repeated the story of what had happened to Oliver.

"I'm afraid," said Fagin, "that the boy may say something that will get us into trouble."

"That's very likely," said Sikes with an evil grin. "The game's up for you, Fagin."

"And I'm afraid," continued Fagin, "that if the game was up with us, it might be up for a good many others. Things might be rather worse for you than they would for me, my dear."

Sikes turned fiercely on Fagin, but the old gentleman merely shrugged his shoulders. There was a long pause before Sikes finally muttered, "Somebody's got to find out what happened at the magistrate's office."

Everyone nodded, but no one wanted to go near a police station under any circumstances. At that moment, Bet and Nancy walked in.

"Nancy, my dear," said Fagin in a soothing manner. "You'll go, won't you?"

"She'll go, Fagin," answered Sikes for her.

Having no choice, Nancy set out with a clean white apron tied over her gown, to find out what she could about Oliver. No one was pleased when Nancy returned with the news that Oliver had been taken to the home of the old gentleman at the bookstall, and not charged with anything.

"We must know where he is, my dears," said Fagin greatly upset. "I must have him found. Go out, all of you, and find him for me, and then I'll know what to do with him." Then he muttered to himself, "If he means to blab about us to his new friends, we may stop his mouth yet."

Trivet
This was a raised metal stand on which a kettle or pot could be placed when cooking over an open fire.

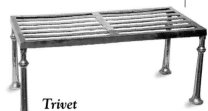

Belcher handkerchief
A famous boxer of the 19th century was named Jim Belcher. He always wore a scarf with white spots on it that became known as a "Belcher Handkerchief."

"Go out, all of you, and find him for me."

There was its living copy.

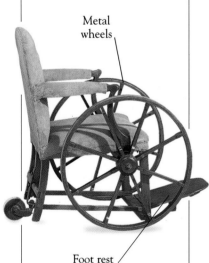

Metal wheels

Foot rest

Wheelchair
Victorian wheelchairs were heavy and cumbersome. This is why Oliver is not able to wheel the chair himself and needs Mrs. Bedwin to push him. Modern chairs are made of lighter materials.

Chapter five

M R. BROWNLOW'S TRUST

WHEN AT LAST Oliver woke, he was very weak and thin. "Where am I?" he asked, feebly. The curtain around his bed was quickly drawn and there stood a motherly old lady.

"Hush, my dear," said Mrs. Bedwin softly. "You must be very quiet or you will be ill again," and she placed Oliver's head gently upon the pillow.

The doctor seemed satisfied with the boy's progress, and after three days, Oliver was able to sit in a wheelchair, well propped up with pillows. Later, Mrs. Bedwin carried Oliver downstairs to a room and sat him by the fireside.

"Are you fond of pictures, dear?" she asked Oliver, seeing him gaze at a portrait on the wall.

"Who is that pretty lady?" he asked. "She looks so sad. It feels as if she wanted to speak to me, but couldn't."

Mrs. Bedwin did not know, but worried that the picture was upsetting Oliver, she wheeled his chair round so that he wouldn't see it.

As she did this, there was a knock on the door and Mr. Brownlow came in.

"How do you feel, my dear?" he asked kindly.

"Very happy, sir," replied Oliver. "And very grateful indeed, sir, for your goodness to me."

"Good boy." He was about to say something more when his eyes fell upon the portrait above Oliver's head.

"Gracious me, Bedwin. Look at this!" He pointed to the picture, and then to the boy's face. There was its living copy. The eyes, the head, the mouth – every feature was the same.

The well-dressed boy
Children of wealthy parents were meant to be seen and not heard. They were dressed in expensive clothes, such as the sailor suit worn by the boy in this photograph, and shown off to visitors.

Oliver soon recovered completely, and the days went by happily and quickly. Mr. Brownlow bought him new clothes, and everything he could want was provided for him. It seemed to Oliver that he was in heaven itself.

One afternoon, Mr. Brownlow was showing Oliver some books in his study when Mr. Grimwig was announced. "Show my friend in," said Mr. Brownlow with a smile.

Once Oliver had left to ask Mrs. Bedwin to bring some tea, Mr. Brownlow asked his friend what he thought of Oliver. "He's a nice-looking boy, is he not?"

"I don't know," said Mr. Grimwig grumpily. "What do you know about the boy? Who is he? What is he? How can you tell if he's honest?"

Oliver set off for the bookstall.

The chance to test Oliver's honesty came sooner than expected. A boy from the bookstall had delivered some books without waiting for payment or for the books that Mr. Brownlow wished to return. At once, Mr. Grimwig suggested that Oliver should go. Oliver himself was so eager to be of help, that Mr. Brownlow allowed him to go, despite his worries for the boy's safety. So, armed with the books and a five pound note, Oliver set off for the bookstall.

"Let me see," said Mr. Brownlow. "He'll be back in twenty minutes, at the latest."

"Oh! you really expect him back, do you?" said Mr. Grimwig. "The boy has a new suit of clothes on his back, a set of valuable books under his arm, and a five pound note in his pocket. He'll join his old friends the thieves and laugh at you. If the boy comes back, I'll eat my head."

On his way to the bookstall, Oliver was just thinking how lucky he was when he was startled by a young woman screaming out, "Oh, my dear brother!" As he looked up to see what was going on, a pair of arms were thrown tightly round his neck.

"Let go of me," cried Oliver, struggling.

"I've found him!" cried the young woman. "Oh! Oliver! Oliver! You naughty boy. Come home now!"

"What's the matter, ma'am?" asked a passerby.

Oliver could do nothing. "He ran away almost a month ago and joined a set of thieves," the young woman replied. "He broke his poor mother's heart."

"It's not true," said Oliver desperately. "I don't know you." Then he saw the woman's face. "Why, it's Nancy!" he exclaimed in astonishment.

"You see, he does know me!" cried Nancy. At the same time, Bill Sikes burst out of a pub, his dog at his heels. "Come, what's this? Young Oliver? Come home to your mother. Here, Bulls-eye," he said to the dog. "Mind him!"

Still weak from his illness, and terrified by the growling dog, Oliver could do nothing.

He was dragged through a maze of dark narrow streets, utterly helpless. The afternoon had turned into a dark and foggy night, when at last they came to a familiar passage and Oliver was pushed roughly into Fagin's lodgings.

"Delighted to see you looking so well, my dear," said Fagin, making a mock bow. "Dodger will find you another suit. You don't want to spoil your best one."

The Dodger smiled as he fished the five pound note from Oliver's pocket.

"That's mine," said Sikes quickly. "Mine and Nancy's for all our trouble in kidnapping the boy. Keep the books, if you like."

Oliver looked dismayed. "They belong to the old gentleman," he cried. "He has been so kind to me. Please send the books and the money back. You can keep me here as long as you like, but please send them back. He'll think I stole them."

"You're right, Oliver. He will think you've stolen them. Ha! Ha!" chuckled Fagin, rubbing his hands together. "Couldn't be better."

Oliver jumped suddenly to his feet and ran from the room, shrieking for help. But it was no use. He was quickly caught and brought back into the room. Fagin picked up a jagged piece of wood from the fireplace and hit Oliver across the shoulder. "That'll teach you to run away," he said. He was about to hit him again when Nancy grabbed the wood and threw it into the fire with a force that sent some of the glowing coals whirling into the room.

"Let the boy alone," she cried. "He'll be a thief, a liar, and all that's bad from now on, just like the rest of us. What more do you want? I wish I'd had no part in kidnapping Oliver." Tearing her hair and dress in passion, Nancy rushed at Fagin but Sikes grabbed her wrists. Nancy struggled in vain, and then fainted.

Fagin looked relieved as Nancy was lain down in a corner. "Charley, show Oliver to bed," he said, wiping his forehead.

Master Bates locked Oliver in a small dark room, but Oliver was too tired to care. Sick and weary, he soon fell sound asleep.

Oliver was too tired to care.

Ladders were used to
reach the lamps.

Lighting up
*The first streetlights in
London were powered by gas
in 1812. By the mid-1840s,
a few years after Oliver
Twist was written, there
were 30,000 lamps in
London. Criminals no longer
had so many dark corners
to hide in.*

Chapter six

THE ROBBERY

THE NEXT DAY Fagin gave Oliver a long lecture. "How could
you be so ungrateful, my dear? And after all we have done
for you in giving you a home." He described how a boy he
had once taken in just like Oliver, told tales to the police and was
hanged on false evidence; Oliver's blood ran cold. Fagin, smiling
hideously, patted Oliver on the head, and went out, locking the
room behind him.

And so Oliver remained for the rest of that day and for many days
afterwards. Lonely and unhappy, Oliver often thought about Mr.
Brownlow and wondered what he would be thinking. Had he known
the truth – that Mr. Brownlow, on advertising for news of Oliver had
met Mr. Bumble; that the beadle had given the worst account of
Oliver's character; and that following this Mr. Brownlow had
forbidden Oliver's name ever to be mentioned again – Oliver would
have been in even greater despair.

It was a chill, damp, windy night when Fagin left his den. He
crept along the slimy, dark alleyways like a lizard, until he reached
a street lit only by a single lamp. Here he found the house that
he wanted.

Nancy and Bill were sitting by the fire when
Fagin came in. Pulling up a chair, Fagin began to talk
about business.

"When's the job at Chertsey to be done?" he asked Bill.

"Not at all," replied Sikes, "unless you can find me a
boy small enough to break into the house."

"Ah," sighed Fagin but, seeing Nancy, hesitated before
saying any more.

"Go on," said Sikes. "You can trust Nancy. She ain't
one to blab."

"Well, then," continued Fagin in a hoarse whisper.
"Oliver's the boy for you. He's small, and it's time he began to
work for his bread."

*Fagin began to talk
about business.*

It did not take long to persuade Sikes to use Oliver for the job, especially after several drinks. And so, to Fagin's delight, it was agreed that Nancy would fetch Oliver the next evening.

"What do you want me to do?" asked Oliver, when Nancy came for him.

"Oh, nothing harmful," replied Nancy. But Oliver could see that Nancy was upset. He knew that she cared for him, and for a moment, he thought about begging her to help him. As if Nancy could read his thoughts, she whispered, "As soon as I can help you I will, but now you must come with me. Give me your hand."

So Oliver took Nancy's hand and followed her to the house Fagin had visited the night before.

"Did he come quiet?" asked Sikes when they got in.

"Like a lamb," said Nancy.

Sikes picked up a pistol and put it to Oliver's head. "If you say one word when you're outside with me, I'll shoot you. Understand?"

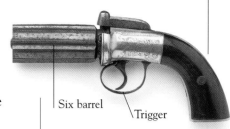

Six barrel | Trigger

Pistol
Most burglars did not carry weapons with them, fearing the death penalty if they were caught. The fact that Sikes possesses a pistol shows what a violent and desperate criminal he is.

Sikes picked up a pistol.

Oliver was woken at half-past five the next morning. It was still dark. Nancy didn't look at Oliver as Sikes pulled him out of the house. He had to run to keep up with Sikes as they crossed London, until at last they were given a lift in an empty cart. They passed several milestones on their way out of town, and Oliver wondered where they were going.

Late that night they reached a large, ruined house. It looked empty, but when they pushed open the door and stepped inside, a loud voice welcomed them. "Bill, my boy, I was afraid you weren't coming. Who's this with you?"

"One of Fagin's boys," replied Sikes. "Now, Mr. Crackit, give us something to eat and drink while we're waiting." This done, they slept for some time until Toby Crackit jumped up declaring it was half-past one. In an instant they had collected all the tools they needed for their work: a pair of pistols, keys, and a crowbar.

The night had turned foggy as they hurried through a deserted little town. The church bell struck two, and they walked even faster until they stopped in front of a detached house surrounded by a wall. Toby climbed it in a twinkling. "The boy next," he said, and before Oliver knew it, he was hoisted over the wall, followed by Sikes.

And now, for the first time, Oliver understood with dawning horror the reason they were here – robbery, if not murder. He clasped his hands together. "Oh, please don't make me steal," he begged. "I promise never to tell anyone anything."

Sikes swore and cocked his pistol.

Toby knocked it from his grasp, put his hand over the boy's mouth and dragged him towards the house, hissing, "I'll kill you myself, if you say another word."

Noiselessly, Sikes forced open a little window at the back of the house. "Now listen, Oliver," he whispered. "I'm going to put you through there. Go along the hall and open the door to let us in. Take this light and go. Now."

Oliver, though deadly afraid, had made up his mind to raise the alarm once inside. Filled with this brave thought, he began to climb in.

"Come back!" Sikes suddenly cried aloud. "Back! Back!" Oliver dropped the lantern, too terrified to move. He saw two half-dressed men at the top of the stairs, then a flash – a loud noise – a smoke – a crash somewhere. He staggered back.

Sikes grabbed Oliver and dragged him through the window. "They've hit him. Look how the boy bleeds!" he shouted.

There came the loud ringing of a bell and men began shouting. Oliver felt himself being carried away.

"Help me carry the boy!" Sikes shouted to Crackit. But Mr. Toby Crackit had no wish to be caught. "It's all up, Bill. Drop the kid and run." They could hear the sound of dogs after them, and Sikes knew Crackit was right. He lay Oliver in a ditch and ran.

Sikes grabbed Oliver.

The house belonged to Mrs. Maylie.

Bow Street Runners
Primarily a detective force, the Bow Street Runners operated from the mid-18th century until 1839, when they were replaced by the Metropolitan Police.

Oliver would have been surprised to see the effect the news of his misfortunes had on Fagin. When Crackit confessed to the evil old man that they had left Oliver, not knowing whether he was alive or dead, Fagin tore his hair out, rushing from room to room crying, "The boy's worth hundreds of pounds to me!" He would have been even more surprised if he had heard Fagin talking about him earnestly to a man whom he called Monks. Why was this man, Monks, interested in his fate?

But Oliver did not know these things. For a long while he lay unconscious in the ditch where Sikes had left him. Even the heavy rain did not stir him. And when, at long last, Oliver did wake, the pain in his arm was so great and he felt so weak that he could hardly move. But he knew he must if he wanted to live.

His head dizzy, and his body shaking and trembling with cold and exhaustion, Oliver staggered forward not knowing where he was going. At last he reached a road and, looking about him, caught sight of a house. Summoning up all his remaining strength, he stumbled toward it. But as he came closer, he recognized the house. It was the same one they had tried to rob the night before! His first thought was to run. But he had no strength left and nowhere to run to. He tottered across the lawn, knocked faintly at the door and then sank to the ground.

You might think that Oliver's luck could not have been much worse – to have arrived, helpless, at the very house that he had been forced to break into. But this time luck was kind to him. The house belonged to Mrs. Maylie, a kind old lady who lived there with her beautiful young niece, Rose. Oliver was taken upstairs and a doctor called for.

"Surely, this poor child cannot be one of the robbers?" exclaimed the old lady, looking at Oliver's sweet face as he lay sleeping.

"He's so young," gasped Rose with tears in her eyes. "Oh, aunt, he may never have known a mother's love, just as I would not have done if you had not given me a home and cared for me like the mother I never knew. Please do not let him be dragged off to prison."

"My dear child," said the old lady. "Do you think I would harm a hair of his head?"

So these two gentle ladies convinced their servants that Oliver had nothing to do with the robbery and had them send away the Bow Street Runners who had been called in to investigate. And when Oliver was well enough to tell them his sad story, they were even more glad they could help this orphan child.

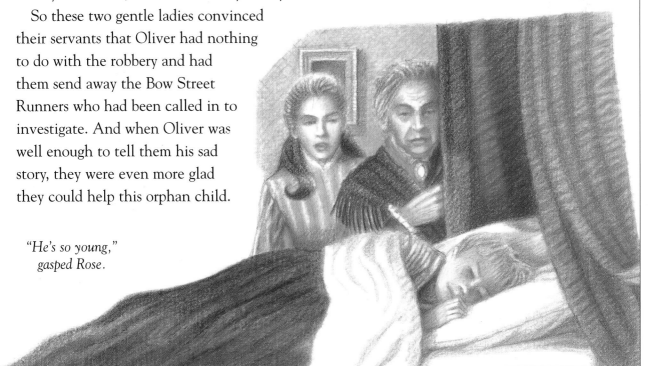

"He's so young," gasped Rose.

Life was so peaceful.

Mary Hogarth
Rose Maylie is based on Dickens's sister-in-law, Mary Hogarth, of whom he was very fond. She died at the age of 17, while Dickens was writing Oliver Twist, *and he was so affected by her death that he included her in his book.*

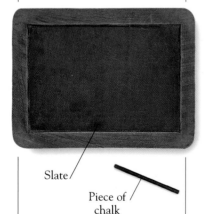

Slate

Piece of chalk

SLATE AND CHALK
Children who were lucky enough to go to school in Oliver's day didn't use pen and paper. They wrote with chalk on a small piece of slate, like a miniature blackboard, that could be wiped clean.

Chapter seven

FACES FROM THE PAST

AS THE WEEKS went by, Oliver grew stronger and happier. Yet he couldn't help feeling a little guilty, too. If only he could find Mr. Brownlow and the kind Mrs. Bedwin who had looked after him before, he could explain his sudden disappearance, and he knew they would be happy for his good fortune now. When, at last, Oliver told Rose what was troubling him, she arranged for him to go to London as soon as he was well enough. And when the day arrived, Oliver could barely contain his excitement. So you may imagine his disappointment when, on finding Mr. Brownlow's house in Pentonville, he discovered that Mr. Brownlow had sold it and moved to the West Indies. Oliver believed his chance of clearing his name had vanished.

However, the Maylies' loving care soon helped ease his sadness. They moved to a pretty cottage in the country, and here Oliver spent happy hours among the green hills and rich woods, watching the spring flowers emerge. Rose gave him lessons every day, and he was an eager pupil. Life was so peaceful and tranquil that Oliver almost forgot the horror of his time with Fagin in London.

But Fagin had not forgotten about Oliver. Quite by chance Oliver had been seen by Monks in the nearby town, and the news that Oliver was still alive made Fagin determined to get him back.

One twilit evening, Oliver was studying in his room and finding it hard to concentrate. The evening sunlight was making him feel drowsy, and soon his head began to nod. In this state of half sleep, he dreamt he saw two faces appear at the window.

"It is him, sure enough. Now we know where he is, let's go," he dreamt he heard the hideous old man whisper.

"I could never mistake him, were he buried fifty feet under the ground. If only he was."

The other man seemed to say this with such hatred that Oliver awoke with a start. And it wasn't a dream. There, at the window, so close he could almost have touched him, was Fagin. With him was a strange man, Monks, whom Oliver did not know except to sense that he was an enemy.

Oliver screamed for help, and the men vanished. But, although the servants searched the grounds, they could find no trace of them.

It wasn't a dream.

A lucky meeting

Pewter tankard

Public houses
Pubs were not considered respectable places and were often frequented by criminals.

Pawnbrokers
Some dishonest pawnbrokers were the recipients of stolen goods. They usually paid a thief a quarter of an item's actual value.

Back at the workhouse where Oliver was born, Mr. Bumble found that his life had taken a turn for the worse. He had been married two months to Mrs. Corney, the matron, and she was always nagging him even though he had been promoted to master of the workhouse. One evening, instead of going home, he wandered into a public house. There was only one other man drinking there.

"I've seen you before, I think," said Monks. "Weren't you the beadle round here once?"

"I was," said Mr. Bumble in some surprise.

Monks smiled and ordered more drinks. "Well, this is a lucky meeting. For I came down here to find you. I want some information and I'll pay you for it." Mr. Bumble listened keenly. Monks wanted to find the old woman who had nursed Oliver's mother. The woman had since died but when Bumble mentioned that his wife had attended the old woman on her deathbed, Monks looked very interested. They agreed to meet again.

At nine o'clock the following evening Mr. and Mrs. Bumble made their way towards a group of seedy little houses near the river. The area was a well-known haunt of criminals. It began to pour with rain, and thunder was not far away. A small door opened and there stood Monks. He showed Mr. and Mrs. Bumble in and led them up a ladder to a dimly lit room.

"Now," he said, addressing Mrs. Bumble impatiently, "tell me what you know about the old woman. What did she say before she died?"

Mrs. Bumble refused to talk until Monks had paid her twenty-five pounds. Then, as a violent thunderstorm shook the house, the matron began her story. "Old Sally confessed to me on her deathbed that she had stolen something from Oliver's mother. She died before she could tell me more, but she was clasping a scrap of dirty paper."

"What did it say?" cried Monks, stretching forward.

"Nothing. It was a pawnbroker's ticket. I took it to the shop and exchanged the ticket for the goods. Here," she added throwing a small leather bag on the table. Monks tore the bag open with trembling hands. Inside was a gold locket and a wedding ring with the word "Agnes" engraved on the inside.

"What will you do with it?" asked Mrs. Bumble. "Can it be used against me?"

"Never," replied Monks. "Nor against me either. Look!" With these words he threw back a large trapdoor at Mr. Bumble's feet. Underneath was the swirling river, swollen by heavy rain. Monks tied a weight to the leather packet and dropped it into the water. "There!" he said, closing the trapdoor. "It's gone. And now it's time for us to go. No one need know anything about what happened here tonight."

"There!" he said.
"It's gone."

Sikes lay ill in bed.

After dark
The night watchman was paid to patrol the streets at night to keep order and to call out the time.

Laudanum
Laudanum was a popular remedy for sleeplessness in Victorian times. It contained opium, a strong drug made from a type of poppy, and was highly addictive.

Chapter eight

A SECRET MESSAGE

BACK IN LONDON, Nancy was sitting sewing by the window while Bill Sikes lay ill in bed with his dog by his side. Illness had not improved Sikes's temper, and he struck Nancy as she tried to help him out of bed.

At that moment, Fagin looked in, followed by the Dodger and Charley Bates. Dodger produced a bundle containing some food and a bottle of wine. Although the food was welcome, Sikes was still angry. "That's all very well, Fagin. But it's money I need."

"I haven't a penny on me," replied Fagin.

"Then you've got lots at home. Nancy shall go and fetch it while I rest here."

After a great deal of haggling and squabbling Fagin agreed to advance Sikes three pounds. Fagin and the boys returned homewards accompanied by Nancy.

"Now," said Fagin, as they reached his lodgings. "I'll go and get you that money, Nancy." Fagin lit a candle and was about to go upstairs when a visitor arrived. It was Monks.

Gesturing to Nancy that he would not be long, Fagin took Monks upstairs to talk privately. Nancy slipped off her shoes and crept to the door, listening with breathless interest.

After about a quarter of an hour, she stole downstairs just before the two men came out of the room. With great reluctance, Fagin handed the money to Nancy and she left.

The next evening, Sikes was still weak from fever and lying in bed. Nancy gave him several drinks laced with laudanum, a powerful sleeping drug, and sat with him until he fell asleep.

Stooping softly over him, she kissed the robber's lips, and then, dressed in her bonnet and shawl, hurried from the house.

A watchman was crying half-past nine. She brushed quickly past him down a dark passage and increased her pace. It was after

Nancy listened with breathless interest.

eleven o' clock by the time Nancy reached her destination: a family hotel in a quiet street near Hyde Park. Nancy hesitated before stepping into the hall.

"Now, young woman!" said a smartly dressed female. "Who do you want to see?"

"Miss Rose Maylie. I must see her," Nancy begged.

A man appeared and pushed Nancy towards the door. "Take yourself off," he said disdainfully.

"Not until you deliver this message!" exclaimed Nancy. "And let me hear the answer."

The man reluctantly proceeded upstairs and Nancy remained, pale and anxious, waiting for the reply.

Chapter nine

OLIVER'S RETURN

"Why did you want to see me?"

S HE DID NOT have to wait long.

"Please tell me why you wanted to see me," said Rose Maylie sweetly when Nancy was shown to her room.

"I am the girl that dragged little Oliver back to old Fagin's on the night he left Mr. Brownlow's house," replied Nancy. " I am the girl who lives among the thieves, and there are those who would murder me if they knew I was here. Do you know a man called Monks?"

"No," said Rose, in bewilderment.

"Well, he knows you and where you were staying. It is because I heard him tell Fagin that I was able to find you. I first overheard Monks talking to Fagin some time ago, on the night when Oliver was forced to break into your house. They were striking a bargain. Monks agreed to give Fagin some money if he could get Oliver back and make him into a thief. I wasn't able to hear any more then. But last night Monks came again. He said that although he'd got the boy's money, he was afraid of Oliver finding out about his father's will and would gladly kill his brother if he could."

"His brother!" gasped Rose. "Oh no!"

"Those were his words. When he spoke of you and the other lady, he said you would give thousands of pounds to know who Oliver really was. I must go back now, it is getting late."

"Back! But if you stay here, I will help you, and then you will be safe."

"I want to go back," said Nancy. "It's hard to explain, but among the men I have told you about, there is one who needs me. I cannot leave him."

"How shall I find you then? This mystery must be investigated to help Oliver."

"Every Sunday night from eleven till twelve, I will walk on London Bridge if I am still alive. And now I must go. God bless you, sweet lady."

Rose found it difficult to sleep that night, wondering what she should do about Nancy's visit. The next morning she was still anxiously considering the matter when Oliver rushed into her room.

"I've seen him, I've seen him!" Oliver cried. "I've seen Mr. Brownlow."

Oliver had written down the address where Mr. Brownlow lived, and Rose arranged for a hansom cab to take them to the house immediately.

Once there, she left Oliver in the cab while she went to introduce herself to Mr. Brownlow and to explain everything that had happened to Oliver.

"He is waiting in a cab at the door," she said.

The old gentleman ran down the stairs to the cab and brought Oliver into the house.

When Mrs. Bedwin entered the room, Oliver flung his arms round her.

"My sweet innocent boy," she cried. "I knew you'd come back."

While Oliver and Mrs. Bedwin chatted happily, Rose spoke privately to Mr. Brownlow about her meeting with Nancy, for she knew she could trust him and that he would know what to do.

Hansom cabs
This Victorian form of taxi had just been invented when Oliver Twist was written. The driver sat at the back of the cab so that passengers got a clear view of where they were going.

"My sweet, innocent boy!"

Nancy started to leave the room.

Chapter ten

A SPY IN THE MIST

O N SUNDAY NIGHT, Nancy was sitting with Bill and Fagin when the church bell struck eleven.

"An hour before midnight," said Sikes raising the blind to look out of the window. "Dark and heavy it is, too. A good night for business."

"Ah!" sighed Fagin. "What a pity, Bill, my dear, that there's none ready to be done."

While the two men were busy talking, Nancy quietly put on her bonnet and started to leave the room.

"Where do you think you're going at this time of night?" cried Sikes.

"I just want a breath of fresh air."

"Put your head out the winder then," Sikes replied, locking the door before pulling Nancy's bonnet off her head and throwing it across the room.

"Tell him to let me go, Fagin," Nancy begged before turning to Sikes again. "Let me go. Just for an hour." She carried on in this way, struggling and crying until the clock struck twelve. And then, as if exhausted by her efforts she stopped.

As Fagin walked towards his house he

pondered Nancy's strange behavior, wondering why she had been so keen to get away. It crossed his mind that Nancy had grown tired of Bill and his brutal ways and had found a new friend. The idea pleased him. Nancy must know that she'd never be safe from Bill's anger if she left him, so perhaps she would agree to poison Bill instead. In a stroke, the man whom Fagin had grown to fear for what he knew about Fagin's long life of crime would be dead and Nancy would be in his power. Nothing could be better. But first he must discover who Nancy's new friend was.

Fagin lost no time in finding a spy. He was unable to call upon the artful Dodger, for the law had finally caught up with him and he had been arrested for picking pockets. The person Fagin chose was Noah Claypole, the very same individual who had made Oliver's life such a misery at Sowerberry's. Noah had robbed the undertaker, taking the money in the till, and run away to London. There he had come to the attention of Fagin who was always on the lookout for useful associates. For the next six nights Noah sat, ready to follow Nancy. But each night, Fagin was disappointed as Nancy did not move. On the seventh night, his luck changed. It was a Sunday.

"She's moving tonight, I'm sure," said Fagin to his spy. "The man she's afraid of is away till daybreak. Come quickly."

They watched as Nancy came out of the door and looked nervously around before moving on. Noah Claypole followed her.

A mist hung over the river on that dark night, deepening the red glow of the fires that burned upon the small boats moored along the banks. The heavy bell of St. Paul's tolled twelve. Midnight had come upon the crowded city.

Nancy saw Rose, accompanied by a gray-haired gentleman, get out of a carriage and walk towards the bridge. She went up to them and whispered, "Not here. It's too public. Come down the steps over there," and she pointed to some stairs leading down to the river.

"That's better," she said when they were hidden in shadows. "Bill stopped me from going out last Sunday. And tonight I feel very afraid. I have had horrible thoughts of death, and a fear that has made me burn as if I was on fire has been upon me all day."

"Imagination," soothed the gentleman. "Now, we want to find Monks and make him tell us his secret, but I must tell you that if we cannot get him, it is very important you tell me how to catch Fagin."

"Fagin?" cried the girl. "Oh no. I could never do that, for even though he's been a devil to me, I will never give him up. I have led a bad life too, and I won't tell on people who never told on me, however bad they are."

"Then," said the gentleman quickly, "tell me how to get Monks."

"But what if he turns against the others?"

"We only want to learn what the man knows about Oliver," said the gentleman. "And I promise Monks will never know how we found out about him."

Reassured, Nancy told him, in a low voice, where Monks could be found, and described what he looked like. "He is tall, with a dark face and sunken eyes. On his throat there is – "

"A broad red mark like a burn?" cried the gentleman.

*A mist hung
over the river.*

"Do you know him?" said the girl
in surprise.

"I think so," he replied. "You have been most helpful.
Tell me how we can help you in return."

Nancy began to cry. "There is nothing you can do. I am chained to my old life.
Though I hate it now, I cannot leave it." Then, looking anxiously around, she said good-bye
and disappeared into the night, followed some minutes later by the astonished listener, who
crept stealthily from his hiding place and darted away to Fagin's house.

Dawn had not yet broken, but Fagin sat wide awake in his lair. His eyes were bloodshot and
his face pale and distorted. He could not believe what Noah Claypole, his spy, had told him.
He felt utter hatred for Nancy, the girl who had dared to blab to strangers. He refused to
believe she would not betray him, and he was bitterly disappointed that his plans to rid himself
of Sikes had failed. Fear of detection and ruin and death consumed him.

At last Fagin heard what he'd been waiting for. The bell rang, and Sikes came through the
door, carrying a bundle of stolen goods which he threw down on the table.

"There's something you should know, Bill," said Fagin, and he woke Noah so that he could
repeat his story.

Sikes listened with a growing anger. Finally, he rushed from the room.

"Bill, Bill," cried Fagin after him. "You won't – be – too – violent, Bill?"

Sikes said nothing, but pulled open the door and dashed out into the silent streets.

He sat in the corner, afraid to move.

Chapter eleven

THE MURDERER

NANCY WAS LYING ASLEEP in her bed when Bill entered the room and woke her.

"It *is* you, Bill!" said the girl, happily. Then she saw, with alarm, the look on his face. "What's the matter, Bill? Why are you looking at me like that?"

"You know what the matter is, you she-devil. You were watched tonight; every word you said was heard."

"Then you'll know that I didn't betray you. I would never do that, Bill. I love you," she cried desperately.

But the robber wasn't listening. He grasped his pistol and was about to shoot when he realized the noise would be sure to give him away. Instead he beat her upturned face with it. She staggered and fell. Shutting out the sight with his hand, Sikes seized a heavy club and struck her down again.

He sat in the corner, afraid to move. Even when the sun came through the window, lighting up Nancy's dead body, he did not stir until he could bear the sight no more. He threw a rug over her, washed himself, and slipped out through the door, dragging his dog with him. Sikes only knew that he had to get out of London.

All day he walked and when he reached the countryside, he wandered on – hiding in ditches and behind hedges when he could. By nine o' clock that evening he was exhausted and his dog was limping. But no matter how far behind he had left London, he could not escape from the image of Nancy's dead body. He seemed to see her shadow in the gloom and hear her clothes rustle in the leaves. She haunted him, following him wherever he went. Finding shelter in a shed he tried to sleep, but even when he closed his eyes he could see her dead eyes in his mind.

Suddenly he heard upon the night wind the noise of shouting. Springing to his feet, Sikes rushed into the open air. The broad sky seemed on fire. The shouts grew louder, and he could hear the cry of "Fire!" mingled with the ringing of an alarm and the crackling of flames. Darting through the undergrowth, Sikes came upon the scene. Half-dressed figures were tearing to and fro, some trying to drag the frightened horses from the stables, others coming laden from the burning building.

Immediately, Sikes plunged himself into the throng of people, now working at the pumps, now hurrying through smoke and flames to help put the fire out. And when morning dawned and nothing but blackened ruins remained, Sikes had neither bruise nor scratch. Some firemen called to him to share their drink, but he could hear others nearby talking about the London murder. He hurried off and walked till he almost dropped upon the ground.

Waking after an uneasy sleep, Sikes decided to return to London. "At least there'll be somebody to talk to there," he thought. "And London's a good hiding place. They'll never think to look for me there. I'll force some ready money out of Fagin and get away to France." Then he looked at Bulls-eye. People would be looking for him, too, he realized. If they saw his dog, they would find him. Sikes decided to drown him and walked on, looking for a pond and a heavy stone. But as if Bulls-eye knew what his master was planning, he ran off when the robber called. Sikes whistled again and again, but no dog appeared. After some time, Sikes gave up and set off for London.

Fire! fire!
Like all road vehicles at that time, fire engines were horse-drawn. Fire brigades were not always efficient. The public often helped put out fires, especially in the country.

HORRID MURDER

Read all about it.
Bloodcurdling tales of real murders were published in special pamphlets. Costing only a penny, they were called Penny Dreadfuls and were very popular.

He seemed to see her shadow in the gloom.

Dirty work
*There were few jobs to be
found in this desperate part
of London. Some made
a living heaving bags of
coal from the ships, as in
this picture. Others turned
to crime.*

Down by the River Thames, in the south of London, there is a place called Jacob's Island. Here the warehouses are empty and falling down, and the houses have no owners. In this dirtiest, roughest part of London only the poorest and most desperate people live. It was here in an upstairs room in a derelict house that three men sat talking.

"When did the police get Fagin?" asked Toby Crackit.

"At dinner time," replied one of the others. "Charley Bates and I made a lucky escape up the chimney."

"And Bet?"

"When she saw Nancy's body she started screaming and raving, so they put her in a straitjacket and took her off to hospital."

The men sat in silence contemplating the terrible events of the last couple of days when Bulls-eye bounded into the room.

"What's that dog doing here?" exclaimed Crackit. "I hope this don't mean Sikes is coming."

Some time later Sikes did appear – or the ghost of Sikes, for his eyes were sunken in his pale head and his cheeks were hollow. No one said anything, till a few moments later Charley Bates came in.

"Charley!" said Sikes, going towards him.

"Don't come any closer, you murderer," answered the boy with horror on his face. "I'm not afraid of you. Kill me if you like, but if the police come here I'll give you up."

They began to fight; then lights appeared below. A crowd was gathering and someone knocked at the door.

"Help! He's here!" cried Charley. "Break the door down."

"Get me a rope or I'll do three more murders," Sikes shouted at the other two men.

The crowd by now had turned into a mob of angry people, baying for Sikes's blood. A huge cry went up when they saw Sikes climb out onto the roof.

"They have him now," cheered a man on the nearest bridge. "Hurrah!" There was another roar from the crowd.

Urged on by the noise below him, Sikes set his foot against a chimney stack and tied one end of the rope tightly round it; with the other he tied a noose to let himself down to the ground. But at the very instant he put the loop over his head to slip under his arms, the murderer looked up and gave a terrified yell.

"The eyes again!" he screeched. Staggering as if struck by lightning, he lost his balance and fell with the noose around his neck. There was a sudden jerk and Sikes was dead, his body swinging, lifeless, against the wall.

Bulls-eye, till now hidden, ran forwards, howling, and jumped toward Sikes. Missing his aim, he too fell to his death.

"They have him now."

Chapter twelve

A NEW LIFE

Locket

These small, ornamental cases were worn around the neck and were very popular in Victorian times. They might be made of silver or gold and usually contained a miniature portrait of a loved one or some other memento such as a lock of hair, as in this picture.

NOW THAT SIKES was dead and Fagin lay condemned in prison, Oliver could almost begin to start his life again, free from fear. But there was still one man he had to meet who would solve the mystery of his identity. And so it was, not two days after Sikes had died, that Oliver found himself going with Mrs. Maylie and Rose and Mrs. Bedwin to the town where he was born. There, in a hotel, Mr. Brownlow met them with a man that Oliver was very surprised to see.

"This is the man I saw with Fagin!" he cried.

Monks looked with hatred at Oliver.

"Yes, Oliver," said Mr. Brownlow gently. "This is your half-brother. And this," he said turning to Monks, "is Oliver. The illegitimate son of your father, my dear friend, and poor young Agnes Fleming who died when Oliver was born. Now you must complete the story."

And so Monks began. "Our father and his wife, my mother, were separated when I was young, and I grew to hate my father. My mother went to see him when he was dying in Paris, and there she found some papers. There was a letter to Agnes asking forgiveness if he should die before they could be married and reminding her of the locket he'd given her and a ring with her name engraved on it."

"And the will," said Mr. Brownlow.

Monks remained silent, so Brownlow continued. "Your father left a will in which he left an income of 800 pounds a year to Monks and his mother. But the rest of his property went to Agnes and their child if it should live and reach adulthood without commiting any unlawful or mean act."

"My mother," said Monks more loudly now, "burnt this will and never sent the letter. She gave it to me before she died, and I promised I would find the child if there was one. When I happened, by chance, to see Oliver with Fagin I knew I could turn him into a

"This is your half-brother."

"There she found some papers."

criminal, and he would not inherit anything."

"The story is nearly over now," said Mr. Brownlow. "But there is one more thing to say. Agnes had a much younger sister she never knew. She was brought up by a kind lady, as if she were her own mother. Monks, do you see Agnes's sister here?"

"Yes, leaning on your arm."

"Oh, Rose," cried Oliver throwing his arms around her neck. "My mother's sister and my aunt. But I could never call you aunt. You will always be my sister." In that one moment he had lost and gained a father, mother, and sister. Oliver did not know how he could feel so much sadness and such joy at one time.

Chapter thirteen

FAGIN'S LAST HOURS

THE COURT WAS PACKED, from floor to roof, with faces. Every eye was fixed on one man, Fagin. When the jury retired to consider their verdict, people began chatting to each other, or eating, or fanning themselves with handkerchiefs.

At last there came a cry for silence, and the jury returned. Their verdict: guilty. The judge ominously donned the customary black cap to sentence the prisoner for his crimes: he would be hanged from the neck until he was dead, the sentence to be carried out on Monday morning. Fagin, a bewildered look on his face, was led away.

As darkness crept into his cell in Newgate prison, Fagin began to think of all the men he had known who had died upon the gallows, some of them betrayed by him. Their faces rose up before him in the dark. Panic-stricken, he beat against the heavy door, crying out for a light. At last two men appeared. One held a candle; the other dragged in a mattress. Fagin lay the rest of the night listening to the church clocks marking off the hours toward morning, the boom of every bell laden with despair. Saturday passed quickly. Then Sunday came, and with it a withering

Their faces rose up before him in the dark.

sense of his own helplessness. He hurried about his cell with gasping mouth and burning skin, consumed with anger and fear. Even the hardened watchmen shrank from him.

Some time before dawn on Monday, Mr. Brownlow and Oliver entered Newgate and were conducted to Fagin's cell.

"Here's somebody wants to ask you some questions, Fagin," said the jailer.

Fagin sat there, muttering to himself, a dreadful expression of rage and terror twisting his face.

"You have some papers," began Mr. Brownlow, "which were put in your hands by a man called Monks."

"It's a lie," Fagin replied.

"For the love of God," said Mr. Brownlow. "Where are those papers?"

"Oliver," cried Fagin. "Let me whisper to you!"

"I am not afraid," said Oliver, letting go of Mr. Brownlow's hand.

"The papers," Fagin hissed in his ear, "are in a bag a little way up the chimney in the top front-room." Then he grabbed the boy. "I want to talk to you, my dear. They'll believe you – you can get me out!"

"Have you nothing else to ask him, sir?" the jailer asked Mr. Brownlow.

"No other question," replied Mr. Brownlow.

They pulled Oliver from Fagin's clutches. Fagin's chilling cries rang in their ears until they reached the yard. It was dawn by the time they left the prison. Already a crowd was gathering around the black stage of the scaffold.

Newgate prison door
Newgate prison was built in 1770. The entrance door – narrow and set within thick stone walls – convinced prisoners that there was no chance of escape.

———•◆•———

Now the tale of Oliver's fortune is nearly told. Mr. Brownlow adopted Oliver, and they went to live in the same village as Rose and Mrs. Maylie, and they were truly happy.

And in the old village church, there now stands a white marble tablet which bears the one word "Agnes," in memory of Oliver's mother – a mother whom he never knew but whose love seemed to protect him even beyond the grave.

In the old village church there now stands a white marble tablet.

DICKENS AND THE THEATER

People were so eager to discover Dickens's latest stories that playwrights adapted them for the stage before they were finished. By the time the last monthly installment of *Oliver Twist* was printed in 1838, there were already six different stage shows of it. The sensational characters and action-packed plot had huge box-office appeal for people of all ages. The theatricality of Dickens's novels is not surprising for he believed that as a writer he was partly a popular entertainer, and he also had a lifelong love of the theater. His readings from his novels were greatly admired. But the strain of acting out such harrowing scenes as the death of Nancy in *Oliver Twist* took a toll on his health. In 1868 he broke down in the middle of a reading tour and died 18 months later. His books have been made into plays, musicals, movies, and TV shows worldwide.

Dickens the actor

It was Dickens's childhood ambition to become an actor, and as a boy he would perform for guests in the family home. When he was 20 he prepared for an audition at the Covent Garden Theater but a bad case of the flu prevented him from going. Soon after that his writing career began.

Dickens took time off of writing to appear in amateur theatrical productions

Palaces of the people

Many new theaters were built especially to accommodate the mass audiences. They were extravagantly decorated, and people liked to dress up in their best clothes to attend them. Dickens's stories, with their heroes and villains, action and adventure and happy endings, particularly appealed to poorer audiences. Like television today, stage adaptations of Dickens's novels were great entertainment and also reflected real social issues.

ALL THE WORLD'S A STAGE

Theater was enormously popular in 19th-century England. The Victorians were particularly fond of melodrama, plays with sensational action and high emotional drama, but there was entertainment to cater to all classes and tastes. Dickens attended pantomimes, puppet shows, musicals and classical theater with equal enthusiasm. In 1860 he wrote that he attended the theater every night.

Great actor managers

This was the age of the great actor/manager – businessmen who produced plays and performed in them. William Charles Macready was one of them and a great friend of Dickens. Another was Herbert Beerbohm Tree, who enjoyed playing eccentric parts. His Fagin was a popular success.

Mr. Beerbohm Tree as Fagin

PERFORMING DICKENS ON STAGE

The vast number of people who were unable to read in Dickens's day were still able to enjoy his stories by seeing them performed onstage. Some audiences of *Oliver Twist* became so violently emotional about Nancy's murder that the Lord Chamberlain, who was responsible for licensing plays for public performance, had to intervene and ban the plays for a short while. Dickens enjoyed watching the adaptations of his books and went to see as many of them as he could.

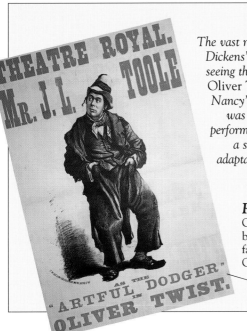

As the Artful Dodger in "Oliver Twist."

Role reversal
Often the part of Oliver was played by a woman. In 1839 Mrs. Keeley, a famous actress, played the part of Oliver at the age of 33!

A poster from one of the many stage productions

Ellen Ternan
Dickens's love affair with the stage spilled over into real life. In 1858 he left his wife of more than 20 years for an 18-year-old actress, Ellen Ternan.

SCREEN AND STAGE

Dickens's novels have appealed to filmgoers since the early days of the cinema. The silent version of *Oliver Twist* in 1912 was the cinema's first serious adaptation of a novel. Many people today have never read *Oliver Twist* but know the story from movies and musicals.

A scene from the 1982 version of Oliver Twist

Artful movie
David Lean's movie of *Oliver Twist* in 1948 with Alec Guiness as Fagin is a classic of British cinema. The black-and-white photography brilliantly conveys the shadow-filled slums and stark emotions.

TV versions
Oliver Twist was made for television in 1982 with an all-star cast attracting new audiences for Dickens's work. This scene shows the artful Dodger being brought before the law.

A publicity poster for the 1948 film

A T-shirt from the stage production

Fagin discusses business with Sikes and Nancy in the 1948 movie version.

The Musical
In 1960, the musical *Oliver Twist* appeared in London with music and lyrics by Lionel Bart. With 2,618 performances, it broke all records as the longest-running British musical, and in 1968 it was made into an Oscar-winning movie. A new production ran in London from 1994 until 1996.

A record cover for the original stage show

OLIVER'S LONDON

Oliver Twist begins and ends in locations outside London, but the heart of the story is set in the crowded capital city after Oliver's meeting with the artful Dodger. Oliver experiences two kinds of life in London: the life of criminals led in the dark alleyways of London's slums where the atmosphere is filled with fear and desperation; and the life lived by wealthy, middle-class Londoners in genteel town houses. The contrasting picture of the two sections of London is dramatically illustrated, and yet they are only streets apart.

Mr. Brownlow's house was in "a quiet shady street near Pentonville."

PENTONVILLE

CLERKENWELL

EVENTS OUTSIDE CENTRAL LONDON

Oliver is born in a nameless town in the Midlands 75 miles (130 km) north of London. He meets the artful Dodger in Barnet, a coaching town near London. Later, Sikes takes Oliver south of London to Chertsey in Surrey to commit a burglary. Here he is rescued and looked after by the Maylies.

The burglary at Chertsey

View of Clerkenwell Green as it was in Dickens's day

CLERKENWELL

This is where the Dodger and Master Charley Bates steal a silk handkerchief from Mr. Brownlow, and where Oliver suddenly realizes the purpose of Fagin's training.

Oxford Street

Long Acre

Waterloo Bridge

SOHO

NELSON'S COLUMN

Strand

The hotel where the Maylies stay in London is near Hyde Park.

MAYFAIR

Piccadilly

Craven Street

HYDE PARK

Sikes takes Oliver on this route out of London for the burglary.

Mr. Brownlow returns from the West Indies to live in a house on Craven Street, near the Strand.

HOUSES OF PARLIAMENT

Westminster Brid

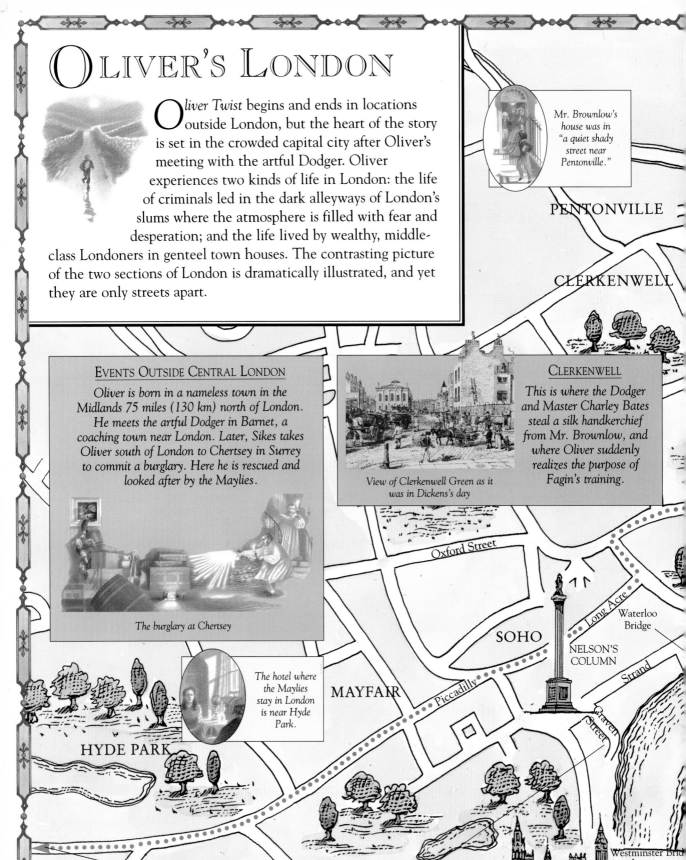

ISLINGTON

Islington Turnpike

ISLINGTON

This was a busy place, being on the main route north out of London. Dodger takes Oliver through the Turnpike, or tollgate, at the end of the Islington road, on their way from Barnet to Fagin's den. Later, Sikes leaves London through Islington after murdering Nancy.

View of the Angel, Islington

"Waking after an uneasy sleep, Sikes decided to return to London."

Angel

After Nancy's murder, Sikes escapes out of London through Islington Turnpike.

St John's Road

Exmouth Street

FAGIN'S DEN

Fagin's den was in Field Lane, in Saffron Hill. It was a notorious criminal hideout in Dickens's time.

A view of Little Saffron Hill

Oliver is taken before the magistrate at Hatton Garden.

Hatton Garden

Saffron Hill
Field Lane

Holborn

Barbican

Long Lane

SMITHFIELD

Finsbury Square

Bethnal Green Road

BETHNAL GREEN

Nancy and Sikes's house was "in the neighborhood of Whitechapel."

Fagin is held at Newgate Prison in the Old Bailey prior to being hanged.

WHITECHAPEL

Whitechapel High Street

Newgate Street

Old Bailey

Fleet Street

ST. PAUL'S CATHEDRAL

Blackfriars Bridge

Southwark Bridge

London Bridge

TOWER OF LONDON

Tower Bridge

LONDON BRIDGE

This is where Nancy secretly meets Rose and Mr. Brownlow, and is spied on by Noah Claypole. The dark recesses of the bridge make a good place for a secret meeting.

Rush hour across London Bridge

JACOB'S ISLAND

Where Sikes meets his death – "near to that part of the Thames on which the church at Rotherhithe abuts…there exists the filthiest, the strangest, the most extraordinary of the many localities that are hidden in London…"

Folly Ditch, Jacob's Island

JACOB'S ISLAND

Acknowledgments

Picture Credits

The publisher would like to thank the following for their kind permission to reproduce the photographs.

t=top, b=bottom, a=above, c=center, l=left, r=right

Barnet Local Studies & Archives Centre: 19b
Bridgeman Art Library, London & New York:
7 (Louis-Jules Arnout 'St. Paul's from Fleet Street,' Guildhall Library, Corporation of London); 18b (W. Duryer & T.M. Barnes 'View of Cheapside, 1823,' Museum of London); 21b (Bonhams, London)
Reproduced by courtesy of the Dickens' House Museum, London: 40tl; 63cl (Little Saffron Hill)
Mary Evans' Picture Library: 2; 8bl; 9tr; cl; bl; 10b;
11t; 15t; 16b; 17t; 26t; 27t; 34t; 38l; 42b; 44c; 53c; 54t; 60tl; tr; br
Ronald Grant Archive: 61cl; cr; bl
Hertfordshire Constabulary: 12tl
Hulton Getty: 8tl; c; br; 9tl; br; 20b; 24t; 31t; 47t; 60bl; 61tr; 62cr; 63tl; bl; br
A. Lamprell: 61br
London Fire Brigade: 53t
Museum of London: 59t
Phillips, London: 13b
Science Museum/Science & Society Picture Library: 30b
David Towersey: 22l; 29t (Bourne End Antiques Centre); c; 42c; 44b; 56t

Additional illustrations: John Lawrence, Sallie Alane Reason